3 0400 00632 215 6

Airdrie
Marigold Library System
NOV 2 5 2011

D0578992

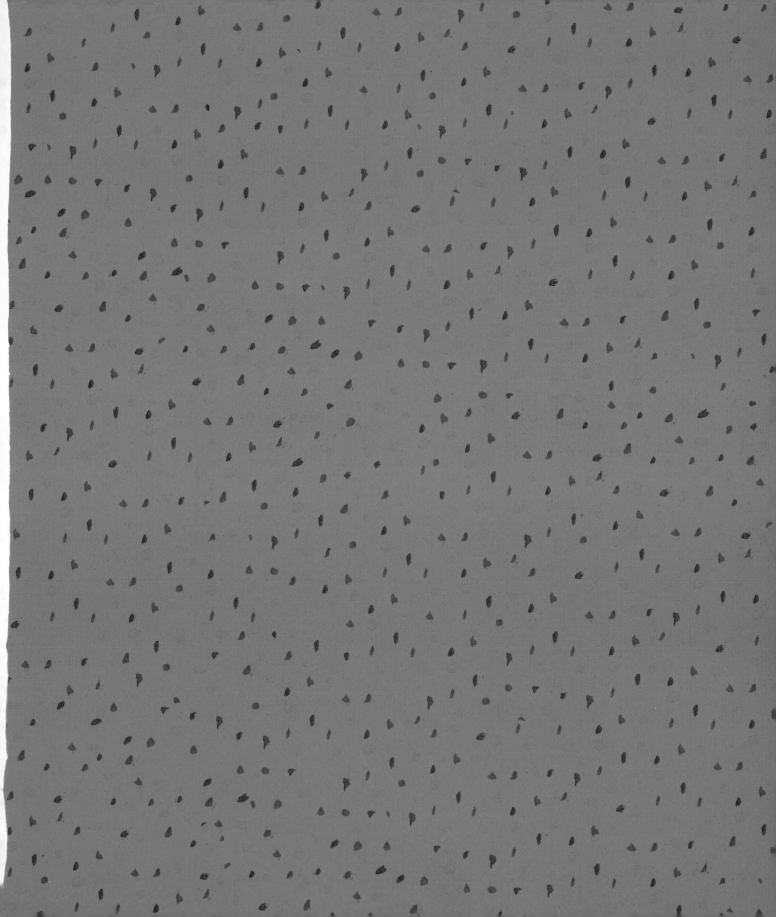

To my parents and older brother,
and also my grandpa, whom I shall miss forever
Y. L.-Q.

Text copyright © 2007 by Yu Li-Qiong
Illustrations copyright © 2007 by Zhu Cheng-Liang

All rights reserved. No part of this book may be reproduced, transmitted, or stored in an information
retrieval system in any form or by any means, graphic, electronic, or mechanical, including photocopying,
taping, and recording, without prior written permission from the publisher.

First published in 2008 by Hsin Yi Publications, Taipei, Taiwan

First Candlewick Press edition 2011

Library of Congress Cataloging-in-Publication Data is available.

Library of Congress Catalog Card Number pending

ISBN 978-0-7636-5881-6

11 12 13 14 15 16 SCP 10 9 8 7 6 5 4 3 2 1

Printed in Humen, Dongguan, China

This book was typeset in Myriad Tilt.
The illustrations were done in gouache.

Candlewick Press
99 Dover Street
Somerville, Massachusetts 02144

visit us at www.candlewick.com

A NEW YEAR'S
REUNION

Yu Li-Qiong

illustrated by Zhu Cheng-Liang

CANDLEWICK PRESS

Airdrie Public Library
111 - 304 Main Street S
Airdrie, Alberta T4B 3C3

Papa builds big houses in faraway places.
He comes home only once each year,
during Chinese New Year.

Today, Mama and I wake up really early because . . .

Papa is coming home.

I watch him from a distance, not daring to get close.
Papa comes over and sweeps me up in his arms,
prickling my face with his beard.
"Mama!" I cry in alarm.

"Look what I've got for you!" Papa rummages in
his big suitcase and takes out—ooh, what a pretty hat!
Mama has a new padded coat, too.

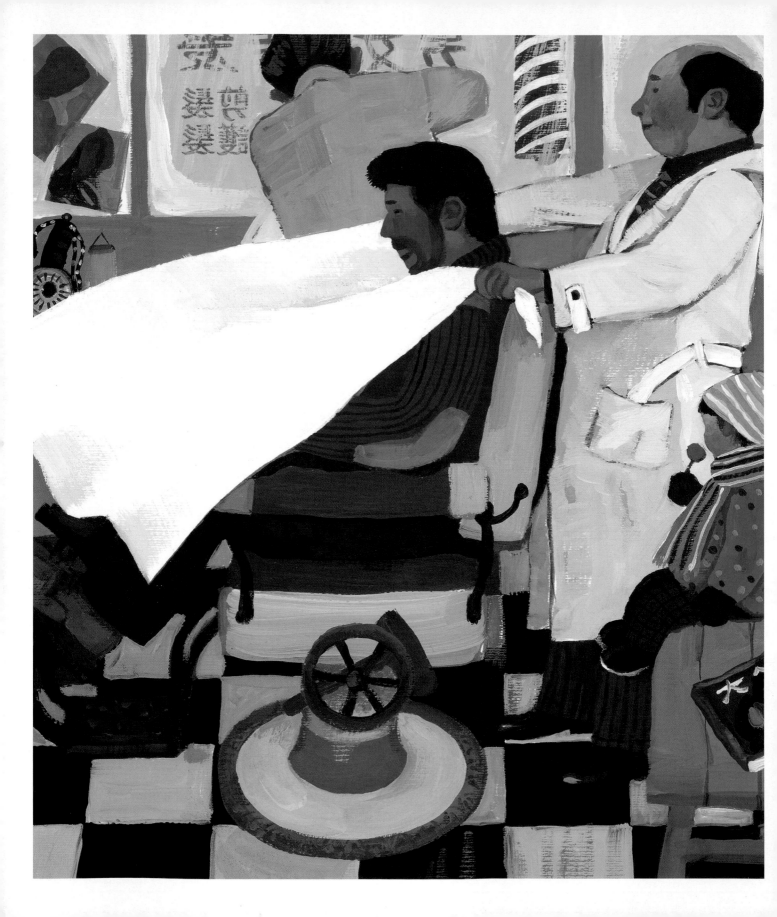

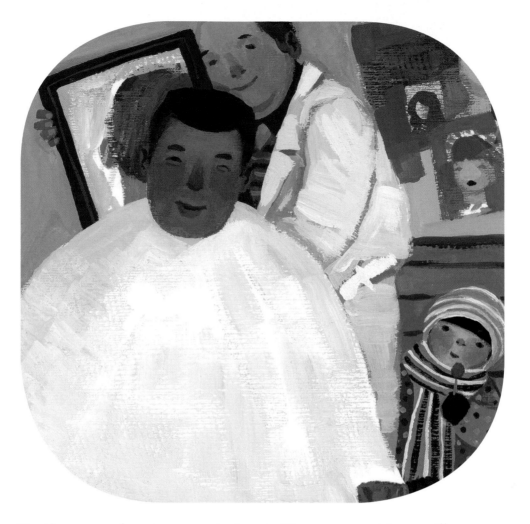

"Let's go and get me a haircut. Then everything will go
smoothly in the coming year," Papa says to me after lunch.
I sit on a chair, waiting.

The Papa in the mirror is getting more like
Papa the way he used to be.

Later, it's time to make sticky rice balls. Papa buries a coin in one of the balls and says, "Whoever finds the ball with the coin will have good luck."

Pop, pop, pop, bang, bang, bang!

We hear firecrackers outside all night.
I lie between Papa and Mama and fall asleep,
drowsily hearing them whispering, whispering. . . .

Early the next morning, Mama serves up piping-hot
sticky rice balls, and Papa feeds them to me with a spoon.
Suddenly, I bite on something hard. "The fortune coin!
It's the fortune coin!" I shout.
"Good for you, Maomao! Quick, put it away in your pocket so
the good luck won't escape!" Papa is more excited than I am.

Mama helps me into a brand-new jacket—
we're going New Year visiting!

On the way, I meet my friend Dachun.

"Maomao, where are you going?"

"I'm out for New Year visits with my papa!"

"Me too. Look, I got a big red envelope!"

"Well, how about this?" I take the coin out of my pocket. "I have a fortune coin! My papa buried it in a sticky rice ball, and I found it!"

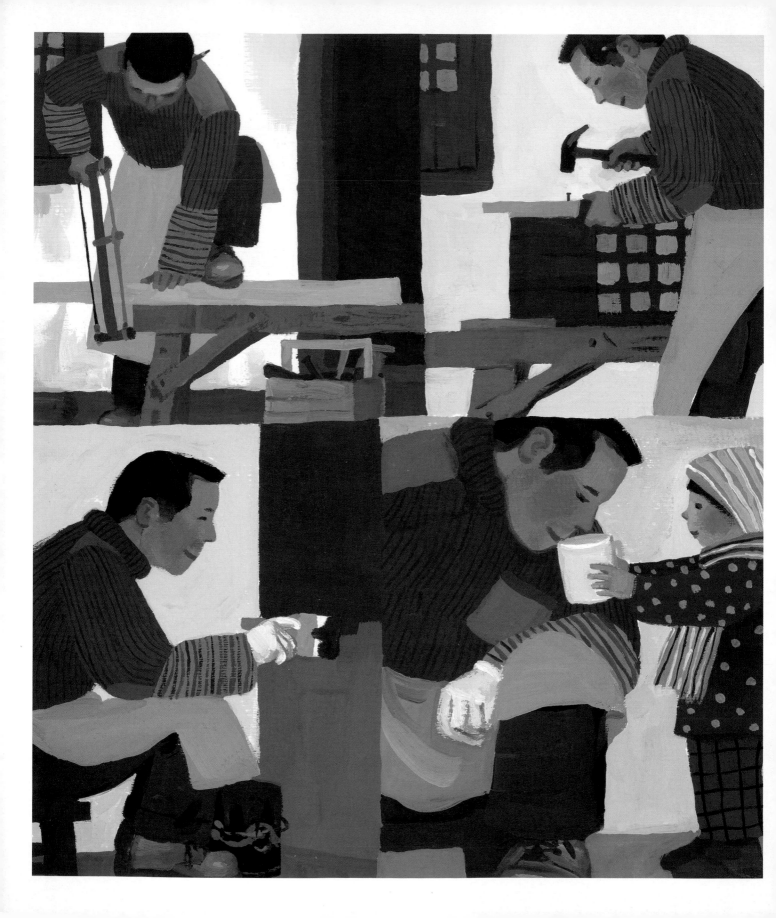

On the second day of New Year's, the sky is gloomy,
and it looks as if it's going to snow. Papa gets busy
fixing the windows, painting the door,
and changing the lightbulbs—
and the whole house brightens up.

"Come on, let's fix the roof!" Papa says with a wink.
Excellent! Mama never allows me up there alone!

Hey, I can see Dachun's roof!
"Listen, what's that sound over there?" I say.
"Oh, it's the dragon dance on Main Street." Papa
straightens up and looks into the distance.
"Where is it? Where is it?" I stand on tiptoe,
stretching up as far as I can.

Papa puts me on his shoulders. "Now can you see it?" he asks.
"Yes, I can. They're coming!"

On the third day of New Year's, it snows—really hard!

When it finally stops, Dachun and the other children come and get me to play. We build a huge snowman in the courtyard and have a snowball fight.

I don't go home till it's getting dark.
I feel inside my pocket and . . . I can't find the coin!
My fortune coin is gone!

I rush out to the courtyard, but it's all covered
in snow. Where is my fortune coin?

"Don't cry, sweetie. I'll give you another one.
Look, it's exactly the same!" Papa scoops another
coin out of his pocket.
"I don't want that one—I want the other one!" I bawl.

In the evening, I creep into bed, miserable, but as I take
off my jacket, *clink!* Something falls to the floor.
It's the coin! My fortune coin!
"Papa, come quick—come and see! I haven't lost
the fortune coin. It's been with me all the time."

That night, I sleep very soundly.

When I get up the next morning,
I see Mama helping Papa pack.
He is leaving today.

Soon, Papa's packing is done. He crouches down
and gives me a big hug, whispering in my ear,
"Next time I'm back, I'll bring you a doll, OK?"

"No, Papa." I shake my head hard.
"I want to give *you* something. . . ."

I put the coin, all warm from being held
in my hand for so long, in Papa's palm and say,
"Here, take this. Next time you're back, we can
bury it in the sticky rice ball again!"

Daddy is very quiet.
He nods and hugs me tight.

Airdrie Public Library